THE ANIMALS OF FARTHING WOOD
Fox's Foe

Colin Dann

Adapted by Clare Dannatt
Illustrated by Gary Rees
Licensed by BBC Enterprises Ltd

RED FOX

'Welcome! Welcome!'

The animals from Farthing Wood had arrived in White Deer Park! They were safe at last, after the dangerous journey to escape from Farthing Wood. Never again would they be driven out of their home by humans, for White Deer Park was a nature reserve.

'Go where you like,' boomed the great White Stag.

'Hooray!' cheered all the animals.

'Fox is our leader forever,' piped up the fieldmice before they scampered off to explore and make new friends.

But in the shadows at the edge of the clearing, another fox watched suspiciously. It was Scarface, the old blue fox of White Deer Park.

'That new fox thinks he's boss,' he muttered. 'But this is MY land.'

The Farthing Wood animals found new homes in trees, under the ground or by the pond, but none of them strayed very far away from each other. They could not forget the promise they had made, before their journey, to help and protect one another, and they still kept that promise.

'We shall have a little Farthing Wood within White Deer Park,' smiled Fox to Vixen.

One morning, Badger woke to see the air filled with snowflakes. Winter had come! The snow fell and fell. It was so cold that even the stream began to freeze. There was little food for the animals and if they hunted too far away, the ugly, scarred face of a strange blue fox sent them running back home with empty stomachs.

Fox grew thinner and weaker until he was no match for Scarface, and so he had to keep out of Scarface's way.

Then Badger woke one day to hear the drip of melting snow and ice. Spring at last!

And with the spring came new-born animals. Vixen watched her new cubs proudly. Friendly wagged his tail as his sister Charmer danced among the tree roots. Bold caught a butterfly and Dreamer wandered about, gazing at the sunbeams.

'You must learn to obey your mother,' barked Fox, 'or you'll run into danger.' But Dreamer wasn't listening.

That evening, a sudden cry from Vixen brought all the animals running. Dreamer was lying on the ground.

'My little Dreamer is dead!' Vixen sobbed over the still body.

'Whoever has done this,' snarled Fox, 'shall live to regret it.'

'It's that Scarface, I know it is!' squeaked Weasel.

Young Bold had listened to his father's words and made up his mind. When no one was looking, Bold trotted off through the forest - towards Scarface's land. Suddenly, Bold heard a horrible snarling noise. He looked up - and found himself nose to nose with Scarface. Bold snarled back daringly. But brave as he was, Bold was still only a cub and couldn't stand up to Scarface.

Soon news was flying back to the Farthing Wood animals: 'Bold has been captured by Scarface! Bold is a prisoner in Scarface's den!'

'I can't be certain that Scarface killed my Dreamer,' said Fox. 'But I know that he has got Bold and I won't let him keep him!' So Fox and Friendly set out to rescue the captured cub.

But before Fox had got anywhere near Scarface's den, Bold managed to escape! He bounded home across the Park but the other animals were angry instead of pleased to see him.

'Your father and Friendly faced great danger to try and rescue you. Scarface caught Friendly and now Fox has had to change places with him so that Scarface will let Friendly go free,' said Owl, who was flying to and fro with news of Fox.

The red and blue foxes faced each other grimly. But there was to be no fight that day, for the great White Stag appeared and stood between them.

'You, Scarface, will let the Farthing Wood fox go. He in his turn will keep to Farthing land.'

Fox nodded in agreement while Scarface looked angry. 'Farthing land!' he muttered to himself. 'I'll show them whose land it is . . .'

Fox sat in the grassy hollow where the Farthing Wood animals liked to meet, thinking sadly about his family and all the trouble Scarface had caused. Dreamer was dead, and Bold and Friendly had both been in serious danger. And now Bold had argued with Fox about how they should treat Scarface and, in the end, Bold had decided to leave the Park.

But Fox had little time to think about his own problems. Suddenly he heard a shriek and a terrified Hare bounded into the hollow.

'Scarface has taken my wife,' cried Hare. 'Do something, please - help us!'

Fox stood and bared his fierce-looking teeth. He had made the same promise as the other Farthing Wood animals and the weaker ones needed his help against this new enemy. What should he do?

Fox paced backwards and forwards. Was it the right time to challenge Scarface? Should he wait and see what the White Stag thought Fox should do, or would that be too late? Scarface was a threat to all the Farthing Wood animals now.

As Fox worried about what to do, he heard Weasel scream, 'Adder's bitten a cub of Scarface's! She's killed one of his sons!'

'Now I have no choice,' said Fox quietly. 'Scarface will want revenge for the death of his cub. He must be stopped - it is him or us! It will come to a fight one day.'

Vixen looked anxiously at her mate. 'You sound a little like Scarface yourself when you speak like that,' she whispered.

'Be quiet!" barked Fox.

Not long after, on a summer's day, Scarface's handsome son Ranger was patrolling his father's land. He caught sight of a red fox cub - nearly on Scarface's land. The cub, who was Charmer, was alarmed and began to run off.

But she looked sweet and harmless in the sunshine and Ranger shouted, 'Don't go! I won't hurt you!'

And so, instead of fighting, the two cubs talked. The more they talked, the more they liked each other.

Charmer ran home happily that night, wondering if she could meet Ranger again. She didn't see that her brother Friendly had been watching her from behind a tree.

Fox decided that the Farthing Wood animals must set up a watch
to guard their land, too, like Scarface.

'I'm ready to help!' said Charmer.

'Some guard she'll be! Charmer's been secretly meeting one
of the blue foxes!' shouted Friendly.

Charmer looked furious. 'Shut up, Friendly,' she muttered.
'It's none of your business.'

'Is this true, Charmer?' asked Fox sternly. 'Because if it is, it could be very dangerous.'

'Yes, it's true,' said Charmer in a small voice. 'But honestly Dad, Ranger won't do us any harm or tell Scarface anything . . .'

'Don't be angry with her,' pleaded Vixen. 'Perhaps the cubs can make peace for us all.'

'We'll see,' said Fox. 'I don't trust Scarface and we'll still have to guard our land.'

Ranger and Charmer met again, but one day they quarrelled.

'I've found out that your Farthing Wood adder killed my brother on purpose,' said Ranger.

'She's a good friend to us and she once saved my Dad's life,' replied Charmer. 'Adder was trying to get rid of your father, not your brother.'

The two cubs glared at each other. Then Ranger sighed. 'Don't let us fall out like your father and mine. We should stay friends,' he said.

And Charmer went home and talked Fox into meeting Ranger the next evening. Fox asked Ranger how Scarface had earned his name.

'A wild cat was terrorising the Park once. But my father soon put a stop to that,' boasted Ranger. 'And that's how he got his scar.'

'We all have our scars,' murmured Fox.

'What would you do if there was war between our tribes?' asked Fox.

'I wouldn't fight for you, but I wouldn't fight against you, either,' declared Ranger.

Fox could see that the young blue fox really meant it. He said goodbye and went home. He was horrified to find Vixen there, wounded - Friendly was licking her torn and bleeding skin clean.

Vixen had met Lady Blue, Scarface's mate, on Farthing land and the two had fought. 'I managed to bite her ear but that only made her fight harder. She knocked me down and bit me as I lay there,' whimpered Vixen.

'Perhaps Bold was right, after all,' said Fox. 'I shouldn't have waited to fight Scarface.'

The animals from Farthing Wood met in the hollow. Hare had brought more news of Scarface and his tribe.

'He said he would defend Lady Blue. He's going to get all the blue foxes together and they'll come to kill us all!'

'We came to White Deer Park to get away from trouble - and now look what's happening!' squealed Weasel.

'I will defend my friends to the death,' cried Fox.

All the animals were silent for a moment, remembering the promise they had made.

Suddenly, a blue fox crossed into Farthing land and ran straight at the patrolling Friendly! He snarled in alarm - but it wasn't Scarface, only Ranger.

Gasping for breath, Ranger cried, 'I must tell you - you're in terrible danger. My father has sworn to kill you all, and he and the tribe are on their way here now!'

'Scarface is coming! Scarface is coming!' shrieked the rabbits, dashing about in a panic.

'Get into Badger's sett,' ordered Fox.

The animals all huddled together underground. Then they listened in terror to the sound of a fox creeping towards them along the tunnel.

'Ranger!' cried Fox as the animal appeared. 'I hoped you would keep your word.'

'I am keeping it,' whispered Ranger. 'I'm going to tell my father that there's no one in here - that the sett's deserted.'

But it was too late. 'I know you're all in there,' snarled Scarface from above. 'Come on out, Ranger, you're no good. I'm going to finish them off myself . . .'

Fox bared his teeth, and ran out of the sett to face Scarface.

'I challenge you to fight me alone,' he growled. 'If you win, the Park is yours. If I win - you will never trouble the animals from Farthing Wood again.'

The two foxes circled around each other. The rest of the animals crept out of Badger's sett. Scarface's tribe crouched opposite them. Charmer saw Ranger at the back, looking very miserable.

Suddenly, Scarface leaped on Fox, and knocked him sideways. Fox scrambled up and rushed at Scarface. The two foxes would fight to the death.

'Come on, Fox!' yelled the Farthing Wood animals.

Then, as the two foxes battled on, Kestrel cried, 'The warden is coming!'

Fox had Scarface pinned to the ground. He knew he could kill his old enemy, before any well-meaning human reached them.

But suddenly Fox just let go of Scarface and turned away. 'I don't want to be a killer like him,' said Fox to his friends.

The Warden tried to help Scarface but Scarface just snarled, picked himself up slowly, then limped off through the trees.

'Scarface will never trouble us again,' Fox told the others.

All the animals knew that the old blue fox was beaten. Now the animals from Farthing Wood could enjoy the peace of the Park they had travelled so far to find.

A RED FOX BOOK
Published by Random House Children's Books
20 Vauxhall Bridge Road, London SW1V 2SA

A division of Random House UK Ltd
London   Melbourne   Sydney   Auckland   Johannesburg
and agencies throughout the world

First published by Red Fox 1994
Text and illustrations © Random House UK Ltd 1994

Based on the animation series produced by
Telemagination/La Fabrique for the
BBC/European Broadcasting Union
from the series of books about
The Animals of Farthing Wood by Colin Dann

Printed in Slovenia
by Mladinska Knjiga

Random House UK limited Reg. No. 954009.

ISBN 0 09 937001 8